The Hand of the Viking Warrior

The Hand of the Viking Warrior

Illustrated by Helen Flook

A & C Black • London

First published 2010 by
A & C Black,
an imprint of Bloomsbury Publishing Plc
50 Bedford Square, London, WC1B 3DP

www.bloomsbury.com

Text copyright © 2010 Terry Deary
Illustrations copyright © 2010 Helen Flook

ISBN 978-1-4081-2239-6

A CIP catalogue for this book is available from the British Library.

This book is produced using paper that is made from wood grown in
managed, sustainable forests. It is natural, renewable and recyclable.
The logging and manufacturing processes conform to the
environmental regulations of the country of origin.

Printed and bound in Great Britain
by CPI Group (UK), Croydon, CR0 4YY

3 5 7 9 10 8 6 4

Chapter One
The Skraelings

North America, 1009

"Don't go too far, or the Skraelings will get you," Freydis told her children.

The fair-haired girl, Irpa, glared at her mother. "I've never seen a Skraeling. You're lying."

Her brother, Skirnir, looked at her, wide-eyed. "You can't call Mother a liar, Irpa, she'll be angry."

Freydis shrugged. "I don't have to get angry. One day, Irpa will be snatched by the Skraelings and they'll eat her. And as they roast her over the fire, Irpa will remember what I told her. Then she'll be sorry. But of course, it will be too late, won't it, Irpa?"

The girl's scowl was as dark as the forest beside the village. "I have never seen a Skraeling," she said, stubbornly.

"That's because they hide so well," Skirnir said. "They dress themselves in branches so you can't see them in the woods. But if you walk past a bush, suddenly it will hop out and get you."

"Hop?"

"Yes, Skraelings only have one leg. Everybody knows that." Skirnir said.

"I didn't know that," Irpa said. "If they only have one leg, then I'll run away. I'm the fastest runner in the village. Even the boys can't beat me."

Freydis slowly stirred her pot of soup and shook her head. "The Skraelings have bows and arrows. They are better than our Viking bows, and twice as deadly. You might run faster than a Skraeling, but you can't run faster than a Skraeling arrow."

"You can't run faster than a Skraeling arrow," Skirnir repeated. He turned to his mother. "Tell Irpa what happened to Thorvald Ericson, Mother. Tell her."

The woman wiped sweat from her brow and walked out of the hut into the warm afternoon air. Her children followed her. Hunters were bringing a dead moose. "The village will eat well tonight," Freydis said.

"It's better than eating squirrels. I'm sick of eating squirrels," Irpa said.

"Tell us the story," Skirnir said impatiently.

The three sat on the grass and bent their heads forward. "It started with Eric the Red, of course," the woman said. "The great Viking warrior was sent away from Norway. Banished."

"He killed a man," Skirnir added.

"He killed *several* men," Freydis said. "He killed Torgest in an argument about a shovel. Then he killed Valthjof in a row about some slaves. Anyway, Eric the Red set off in boats with sheep and cattle and about a hundred friends and family. They sailed west, on past Iceland until they came to Greenland. And that's where they settled."

"Were there Skraelings in Greenland?" Skirnir asked.

"Oh, yes. But they were friendly ones ... with two legs," Freydis explained.

"So why did we leave Greenland and come here?" Irpa asked.

Freydis sighed. "Greenland isn't very green – Eric just *called* it Greenland so other Vikings would sail from Iceland to settle there. Eric's son, Lief, set sail to find some *really* green land and he came here to Vinland." The woman looked over the fields. "Here the grass grows, even in winter, for our cattle. There is wood to build houses and boats. There are wild animals and berries and nuts in the forests. It is perfect."

"Except for the Skraelings," Skirnir said.

"There *are* no Skraelings," Irpa repeated.

"Don't forget what happened to Thorvald," said her mother.

"What did happen to Thorvald?" Irpa said.

Chapter Two
The Arrows

"Thorvald's brother, Lief, arrived here and met the natives," Freydis continued. "They made a lot of frightful screams, so Lief called them Skraelings ... screechers. But they didn't attack the Vikings that year."

"But they *did* attack," Skirnir said. "Tell us what happened when they attacked, Mother."

"It was three years later, and Thorvald had arrived in Vinland. Early one morning, a Viking saw a Skraeling watching them. The Skraeling was covered in bear fat to keep out the cold, and he shone in the sun. The Vikings shouted at him and he ran away..."

"On one leg?" Irpa scoffed.

Her mother ignored her. "The Vikings ran after him and they came across nine Skraelings. They were camped out at the edge of a lake. They were sleeping.

"Thorvald decided to attack the natives before they could pick up their weapons. Eight were killed. But the ninth escaped and ran for help."

"Why did Thorvald attack them?" Irpa asked.

"Because he was a fool," Freydis sighed. "The Vikings and the Skraelings could have lived in peace. But now Thorvald had started a war. And of course he was the first to die in the war."

"The Skraelings shot him, didn't they, Mother?" Skirnir said.

"They did. They shot him in the guts with an arrow. His friends carried him back to camp and fed him porridge and onions."

"Porridge and onions?" Irpa laughed. "That's foul. Why did they do that?"

"The porridge went into his guts, of course. They pulled out the arrow and what do you think they could smell?"

"Onions," Skirnir said. "That meant the arrow had gone through his gut. There was no hope for him."

"Thorvald said, 'This is a rich country we have found; though I will not enjoy it.' He died a few hours later," Freydis said.

"Who won the war?" Irpa asked.

Her mother shook her head. "It's still going on."

"I haven't seen any Skraelings," Irpa argued.

"We've only been here a few months," her mother told her. "But some of our hunters say they've seen shadows in the trees – eyes watching – bodies covered in bear fat shining in the distance."

Skirnir shuddered. "The first time you see a Skraeling could be your last, little Irpa. One day, you'll wander too far from the village and they'll get you."

"Go into the fields and weed the corn," Freydis said. "You'll be safe in the fields. Just stay out of the woods."

"Go in the woods," Skirnir hissed. "Go on. I dare you."

"Skirnir!" the woman said sharply. "Don't tease your sister. Now go and help her weed the crops."

"Aw, Mother! I want to practise fighting with the men. I want to be a warrior, not a weeder."

"You will be a warrior with a slapped ear if you don't start weeding. Now!"

Skirnir ran.

Chapter Three
The Visitors

The Skraelings came that night.

The Vikings woke to find a band of twenty native warriors standing on the hilltop above the village. They were armed with bows, but the bowstrings were left slack. The natives were not planning to attack.

Skirnir and Irpa ran to the edge of the village where the Viking men were gathered, stirred from their sleep by the watchman.

Most of the men carried swords and shields. Karlsefni, the Viking chief, looked up the hill silently.

"Skraelings!" Skirnir squeaked at his sister. "You said there were no Skraelings. See? There they are."

"They have two legs," Irpa said.

"Yes – they're two-legged Skraelings."

Irpa sneered. "So are two-legged ones more dangerous than the one-legged ones?"

"Probably," Skirnir said. "They can kick you without falling over."

"Be quiet," Karlsefni said.

"Yes, be quiet," Skirnir told Irpa.

"I was speaking to *you*, Skirnir," the Viking leader growled.

"Sorry, Karlsefni," the boy muttered.

Karlsefni stroked his thick, yellow-grey beard. He watched as the natives on the hill placed their bows on the ground. "Put your weapons down," the Viking chief said.

"Are you mad?" one of the men argued. "They could be carrying knives. When they get close they could cut our throats!"

"They are carrying furs ... see?" Karlsefni said. "They've come to trade."

The natives walked steadily down the hill towards the Vikings. One of the natives held out a bearskin to Karlsefni. The Viking looked at it and threw it round his shoulder. "It will be good in winter," he said. "What do you want in return?"

The native shook his head. He did not understand. He stepped past Karlsefni and walked around the wooden huts where the women and children were looking out of the doors. The native picked up some red woollen cloth and wrapped it around his head. He smiled. He pointed to the bearskin and he pointed to the cloth.

"Swap?" Karlsefni guessed.

"Sop," the native nodded.

For the next half hour, the natives wandered through the village offering furs for clay pots, iron knives, silver brooches and buckles, leather pails full of milk and cheeses wrapped in cloth.

"Sop!" they said and the Vikings were usually happy to take the rich furs.

At last the natives had no more furs and they turned to walk back up the hill carrying their traded goods.

And that was when it all went wrong.

Chapter Four
The Bull

The Viking cows grazed in the open plains. But Karlsefni's bull was kept in a wooden pen by the path. Lief Ericson had brought it across in a boat when the animal was a calf. In the rich grass of Vinland, the bull grew older and stronger, with a temper as fierce as Thor himself. His sharp horns could toss the largest Viking in the air and his huge hooves could crush him as he fell to earth.

Now a native saw the shining ring in the bull's nose and walked off the path to look at it.

As he reached for the ring, Karlsefni cried out, "No!"

Too late. The native tugged at the ring. The bull was furious. It lowered its head and charged at the fence. The wooden rails creaked and cracked. The bull stepped back to give itself a run at the fence. The second time the rails snapped and the bull was free.

It snorted and looked down at Karlsefni and the families in the village. The Vikings prepared to run and hide.

The natives were running for their bows that they'd left at the top of the hill. When they reached their weapons, they began firing arrows at the animal.

Some arrows struck its thick hide and pricked it, but didn't do much harm. The bull decided the natives were more annoying than the Vikings. It lumbered up the hill after them.

The natives ran. When they had a chance, they turned and fired. Arrows rained down on the village as Skirnir and Irpa ran to hide under the thatched roofs of the huts.

"They are terrible shots," Skirnir cried to his sister. "They aren't getting anywhere near the bull."

Irpa shook her head. "They aren't aiming for the bull – they are aiming for us," she told him.

"She's right," Karlsefni said, as he held his shield over their heads.

"Why?" Skirnir asked.

"Because they think it's our fault. They probably think we keep that wild animal to attack our enemies."

"That's mad," Skirnir groaned.

"Maybe. But it won't save us. Remember what happened to Thorvald."

"The natives came back with an army of warriors," Irpa said. "Is that what these natives will do?"

"I think so," Karlsefni said. "But we are farmers. We can't fight off a band of warriors. They'll kill us all."

"I don't want them to kill me!" Skirnir wailed.

"Then there's only one safe place," the Viking chief said.

"Where?"

"Greenland."

Chapter Five
The Wolf

The Vikings sat around the roasting deer. It was a fine feast but no one looked happy.

"We can't just run away," Freydis argued. "We came from the cold, grey rocks of Greenland to find a really green land. We could have a good life here."

Karlsefni nodded. "Then here is what we'll do. We'll wait and see if the Skraelings return. If the same group comes back, we'll defend the village."

"And if they bring a huge army?" one of the farmers asked.

"Then we'll go down to the boats and sail home to Greenland. Let's start packing the boats," the chief said.

The Vikings ate quietly for a while.

"We need a guard," Freydis said. "We need a warning. It will take us time to get to the boats, driving the sheep, carrying as much as we can on carts."

The other Vikings agreed to take turns to watch from a hilltop day and night. If they saw a large Skraeling army, they would warn the village and flee.

"But we can't outrun the Skraelings," Freydis argued. "We are slow as that bull. If they catch us, we'll never get home."

Karlsefni stared into the embers of the fire. "Remember Fenrir?"

"Ahhhh!" the farmers sighed.

"Who's he?" Skirnir asked.

His mother turned to him. "Fenrir is a wolf," she said. "The mightiest creature in the world. His jaws are so strong and wide they could eat a giant."

"He doesn't live in Vinland, does he?" Irpa asked. "I've never seen him."

"He lived in the forest Jarnvior. The gods decided that Fenrir had to be chained up to stop him eating everything," the woman went on.

"But he would eat the person that tried to chain him!" Irpa gasped.

"He would. So the gods played a trick. They said, 'Fenrir, show us how strong you are. See if you can smash this chain.' And the wolf let them fasten a mighty chain around his leg."

"And then he was chained up?" Skirnir said.

"No. He smashed that chain and then he broke free of an even stronger one. So the gods had a chain made of silk."

"Silk?"

"Silk and magic. It was made by dwarves. They asked Fenrir if they could fasten it around his leg. But Fenrir thought it might be a trick. He said, 'Fasten it around my leg. But one of you gods must place an arm in my mouth. If the chain is a trick, then the god will have his arm chewed off.' Fenrir had to be chained. Only one god was brave enough to place his arm in the wolf's mouth. The god Tiw."

"What happened?" Irpa whispered.

"They fastened the silk chain to Fenrir's leg. No matter how much he struggled, he could not get free. So he snapped his jaws shut in a rage and chewed off brave Tiw's hand."

"Tiw lost a hand?" Irpa said.

"But he saved the world. Fenrir is fastened by Lake Amsvartnir, and there he will stay for the rest of time."

Irpa frowned. "But how does that help us in a fight against the Skraelings?" she asked.

"I think I see what Karlsefni wants. He wants one of us to risk our life to save the whole village. Isn't that right, Karlsefni?"

"It is," Karlsefni agreed.

Chapter Six
The Broken Cart

Karlsefni took a stick from the fire and drew a simple map in the ashes. "We are here in the village. The boats are to the east ... and the Skraelings will attack from the west.

"As we march east, they will chase us and catch us, just as Freydis says. But here ... to the north ... is the forest." He scrawled a tree in the ashes.

"If we can get the Skraelings to go searching in the forest, it will give us time to reach the ships," Freydis said.

The Viking chief pointed at his map. "When our watchman runs and tells us the Skraelings are coming, we will head east. But one person will head north on the path to the forest. We'll give them a cart loaded with some food and farm tools. The cart will have a broken wheel."

Irpa clapped her small hands. "The Skraelings will think we've run to hide in the forest. They'll see the broken cart and think this one has been left behind."

Her brother Skirnir was just as excited. "The man with the cart can shout into the woods ... pretend he's calling out ... warning us the Skraelings are headed that way."

The villagers started to smile until Freydis cut in. "But who will stay with the cart?" she asked. "Who will be our Tiw and risk their life to save the others? When the Skraelings catch him, he will die."

Karlsefni shook his head. "The Skraelings may not catch him." He jabbed at the map again. "Look ... as soon as the Skraelings head for the woods, our man will leave the cart and run into the trees. He'll have a good start on the enemy. The Skraelings will be running uphill and carrying their weapons. If our Tiw is fast enough, he can disappear into the trees."

"But he can't live there for ever. The bears or the snakes will get him in the end," a farmer sighed.

"No. Once he is in the trees, he can turn east and make for the seashore. The Skraelings will be searching the trees for us. Our man can pop out where the forest meets the beach. He can jump on the last ship. He will be saved ... we will all be saved."

Freydis chewed on a bone and thought. "It will have to be someone as brave as Tiw and as fast as the wind," she said.

Karlsefni looked around the circle of Vikings. "If the Skraelings return in force – and I think they will – we need a brave, swift runner to make our plan work. I want one of you to step forward if he thinks he can be our great Tiw."

The farmers looked at the meat in their hands, or at their knives, or into the ashes, or looked up at the birds overhead. No one met the eyes of Karlsefni. A farmer muttered, "I would do it but my family need me to pull our cart."

His wife said softly, "I would do it, but I'm too slow – I got a thorn in my foot yesterday."

At last, young Skirnir stepped forward.

Karlsefni grinned. "Skirnir!" he cried. "This brave lad shows us the courage of a true Viking. Skirnir? You will stand by the broken cart and lead the Skraelings away?"

Skirnir shook his head. "No, I was just going to say ... the job should go to the fastest runner in the village. They would have the best chance."

"And that is you?" Karlsefni asked.

"No, it's my sister ... Irpa."

Chapter Seven
The Attack

Irpa didn't sleep that night, or the night after. Her brother had put her in this danger. She was angry with him and afraid of the Skraelings.

She tried not to show it to the others. The villagers had cheered for her and given her gifts of honey cakes and a shawl of finest wool. "Our Tiw," they called her.

At the second sunrise, the watchman ran into the village. "The Skraelings are coming!"

"How many?"

"Two hundred or more."

The villagers dressed quickly and loaded their carts. They gathered their animals and began the slow walk east to the ships.

Freydis gave her daughter a crushing hug. "Be brave, my Tiw ... and I'll wait for you on the last boat to leave."

"I'll wait, too," Skirnir said.

"Thank you," Irpa said bitterly.

As the last villager left the village, the girl ran up the hill to where the broken cart was waiting. To the west, she saw a cloud of dust and two hundred marching Skraelings.

When they reached the ridge to the west of the village, Irpa began to scream at the trees, "Run, my friends. Run! The Skraelings are coming ... run and hide in the trees! And I am making lots of noise because the Skraelings won't understand anyway!" she added.

The Skraeling scouts looked towards her. They put their heads together. Half of the native warriors were sent to search the village. Irpa trotted towards the trees.

At the edge of the forest, she looked back one last time. The huts were burning and the army had turned towards her.

Irpa ran.

The paths were soft and damp and her bare feet sped along into the green gloom. Angry voices sounded behind her. They sounded close.

She reached a clearing where the sun broke through to the forest floor. It was morning so the sun would be in the east. If she kept the sun ahead of her, she would reach the ships.

Irpa turned. There were fewer voices now. She slowed and looked back. Then, between the trees, she saw a single Skraeling. He was fifty paces away. He was not much older than Skirnir. Even if he caught her, he couldn't hurt her much.

But the boy turned when he saw her. He let out a screech that would make the blood of Karlsefni's bull run cold. That would bring the whole army after her.

The boy was as quick as a deer. Irpa knew she couldn't head east. She would lead the Skraelings straight to the Viking ships.

"What would Tiw do?" she moaned.

Irpa turned north again. The change worked. The boy lost sight of her. Irpa slowed to a walk so her feet wouldn't make a sound on the dry, fallen branches. She heard older warriors arrive and talk to the boy.

Then there was the scurry of squirrels behind her. Someone had scared them. Someone was coming her way. Irpa turned and ran north.

Chapter Eight
The Forest

Irpa felt she had run for ever. Then, at last, she came out of the northern edge of the wood. It was quiet here on the grassy plain. To the east she could see the ocean sparkling in the morning sun.

She had run so far the Vikings must be safely away by now. She trotted wearily down towards the coast.

A westerly breeze was blowing at her back. She saw it filling the sails of a Viking ship as it headed back to Greenland. She knew there were four ships – she had helped to load them the day before.

A second ship drifted silently past and she was still a mile away. Then she saw the third ship following and she thought her heart would stop. They were leaving without her!

She remembered Tiw. Yes, he'd saved the world, but it had cost him a hand. Irpa had saved the villagers of Vinland, but it might cost her a life.

The land sloped steeply towards the beach. She could see the last boat, pulled up on the shore. She tried to run, but the sand was soft and seemed to suck down her weary ankles.

Where the sea lapped at the sand, it was firmer. Irpa splashed through the cool water. She raised her head and saw the sail being raised. Her friends hadn't seen her.

"Wait!" she screamed.

The sail stopped, then began to lower. Irpa ran on.

"Hurry!" the Vikings called. They were pointing.

The girl looked over her shoulder. The Skraeling boy had reached the shore. He was running after her. He was stronger than she was. He was catching her.

Suddenly, a cloud of arrows rose from the Viking boat, sailed over Irpa's head and sank into the sand around the boy. The native stopped. He pulled an arrow from a pouch at his back, loaded the bow and took aim at Irpa.

She watched the single arrow race towards her and she dived into the shallow water. She felt feathers brush her cheek and saw the arrow splash down beside her.

Irpa scrambled to her feet, and as more Viking arrows drove the boy back, she reached the side of the boat. Freydis and Skirnir gripped her wrists as the Vikings hauled the sail up the mast again. The breeze tugged at the boat and it slid into the water.

Irpa turned and looked back at the native. He stood in the shallow water with his hands on his hips. He was panting.

"It was a good race," Irpa cried.

The boy did not speak Norse, but he seemed to know what she was saying. He grinned and waved a hand. Irpa waved back. She watched him till he was as small as a grain of sand.

The forests were a deep green and the plains a softer shade. Freydis sighed. "Back to the icy rocks of Greenland. This is a rich country we have found, as Thorvald said."

"But it isn't *our* rich country," Irpa said.

"No," her mother agreed.

"You said you didn't believe in Skraelings," Skirnir said.

"And you said the Skraelings would get me," his sister reminded him. "But they didn't, did they?"

Epilogue

The Vikings arrived in Vinland, the land we now call North America, around 1001. Many people believe Christopher Columbus "discovered" America in 1492, but Lief Ericson was there about 500 years before him.

The native Americans were peaceful towards them at first. They caught wild animals like squirrels and traded their furs for Viking milk and cloth. But in 1004, Thorvald arrived and started attacking the natives. Thorvald died in the war that followed. His last words were, "This is a rich country we have found;

though I will not enjoy it."

In 1009, a Viking group arrived to settle with their leader Karlsefni. They didn't stay long. One story says the Skraelings were peaceful until they were attacked by Karlsefni's bull. The Vikings gave up trying to settle in America and went back to Greenland. We can't be sure why the last Vikings left. Maybe the wars against the native Americans were too vicious for the Viking farmers and their families. Not all Vikings were warriors.

One strange Viking legend is about Tiw and the wolf Fenrir snapping off his hand. Tiw is a Viking hero and one day of the week is named after him – Tiw's Day – Tuesday.

TERRY DEARY'S KNIGHTS' TALES

THE **KNIGHT** OF SWORDS AND SPOOKS

THE **KNIGHT** OF SILK AND STEEL

THE **KNIGHT** OF SPURS AND SPIRITS

THE **KNIGHT** OF STICKS AND STRAW